Praise for Storyshares

"One of the brightest innovators and game-changers in the education industry."
— Forbes

"Your success in applying research-validated practices to promote literacy serves as a valuable model for other organizations seeking to create evidence-based literacy programs." — Library of Congress

"We need powerful social and educational innovation, and Storyshares is breaking new ground. The organization addresses critical problems facing our students and teachers. I am excited about the strategies it brings to the collective work of making sure every student has an equal chance in life." — Teach For America

"It's the perfect idea. There's really nothing like this. I mean, wow, this will be a wonderful experience for young people." — Andrea Davis Pinkney, Executive Director, Scholastic

"Reading for meaning opens opportunities for a lifetime of learning. Providing emerging readers with engaging texts that are designed to offer both challenges and support for each individual will improve their lives for years to come. Storyshares is a wonderful start." — David Rose, Co-founder of CAST & UDL

Artemis

Storyshares presents

Published by Storyshares, LLC
Inspiring reading with a new kind of book.

Storyshares
Storyshares, LLC
24 N. Bryn Mawr Avenue #340
Bryn Mawr, Pennsylvania 19010-3304
www.storyshares.org

Interest Level: Post-High School
Grade Level Equivalent: 3.4

ISBN 9798885977777
Book design by Saskia Globig

ARTEMIS

Leonard Varasano

CONTENTS

CHAPTER ONE

The long nights were always the worst for the young boy, and this evening was no exception.

This night brought shadows: thick, black gloom covering his room in utter darkness. Death was beckoning, coming closer by the moment. It surrounded his bed, trying to cut off his life from the world of the living.

Though covered with a feverish sweat, the boy shivered violently. He thrashed his head from side to side on his drenched pillow. The boy was a fighter. He'd fought off death before during other long nights, only to have his illness attack him again. It was a vicious cycle that seemed to have only one conclusion.

Tonight was different, though. It was worse than ever. He tried to call his nurse, but he was too weak and couldn't lift his withered arms to click the call button. He felt his life being sucked out. The darkness pushed down in a suffocating, final embrace.

He began to cry, but it was no louder than a whisper. He just wanted to see his parents again, to see their faces once more.

Just once more. Please, please... please?

But the darkness tightened even more, and he felt the end was coming.

"It's all right, Joey."

Through the gloom, the boy saw Artemis now stood beside his bed. Suddenly, he could breathe again.

"Artemis... I'm dying!" he cried.

Artemis dipped a washcloth in a basin of cool water and swabbed the boy's head. "No, Joey," he said. "You're going to see your parents tomorrow. How about that?"

"I will?" Joey asked.

"Yes, you will," Artemis said.

As Joey studied Artemis's gentle face,

waves of calm flowed through his ravaged body. Artemis was his friend, and when he was around there was always a feeling of peace. Especially at night, like now.

Artemis stayed with Joey until his breathing slowed to normal and the boy had finally fallen into a deep, restful sleep.

CHAPTER TWO

The next morning, in the corner of the hospital's consultation room, a young couple huddled together in desperation. They sat across the table from a grim-looking man wearing a white lab coat. He looked at the couple, slowly shaking his head.

"Steve... Kate. There's nothing else we can do for Joey. The cancer has spread throughout his body." He waited for a moment, allowing his words to sink in. "The final stages are quickly accelerating. You should take Joey home while he still has some quality of life..."

At a loss for words, the doctor's voice trailed off. "I'm sorry."

Despite knowing that this day was coming, the couple was still devastated by the sad news. Medical science had done all that was possible for their son.

Steve stared at the floor, holding his head in his hands. Though weary and numb after five long years of hopelessness, he managed to pull himself together to help his family through this darkest of times. Reaching out, he stroked his wife's hair and spoke softly.

"Thank you, Doctor," he said. "We'll find a nurse and prepare Joey."

Kate nodded absently as her husband guided her from the room.

The doctor stood, glancing down at his trembling hands. No matter how many times in his career he'd told parents their child was dying, he'd never gotten used to it. He locked the door and then walked to the window. Staring out, he sighed deeply.

CHAPTER THREE

Holding hands, the young couple followed the quiet corridor toward Joey's room.

Opened doors revealed sleeping children hooked up to monitors and breathing apparatus. An oppressive feeling filled the pediatric ward.

Outside Joey's room, Artemis slowly pushed a utility cart. Smiling as the couple approached, he saw the looks on their faces. He lost his grin, nodding as they came close. He couldn't help but notice the look in the woman's eyes as she dabbed them with a tissue. When Joey's parents entered the room, he lowered his head, then pushed the cart into a closet and disappeared down the corridor.

An hour later, with Joey carefully bundled up and carried by his father, the family left the hospital. They drove off in their pickup truck. It was midmorning and the sunshine was a brilliant, golden light.

Joey was awake, watching the road, the trees, and the sky. He hadn't been outdoors in a long time and was enjoying the break from his routine. Looking at his parents and their tight expressions, he knew something was wrong. But being seven years old, he didn't understand much of the grownup world. Pain had been his teacher. That, he understood too well.

Staring out the window, Kate noticed the elderly man who'd been outside Joey's room, walking slowly along the road.

"There's Artemis, from the hospital. Think he needs a ride?" she asked.

Steve slowed the pickup onto the road's shoulder and stopped, then hopped out of the cab. "Howdy, Artemis."

The old man smiled. "Well, hello there."

"Figured we could give you a lift," Steve said.

"That's very nice, but I usually walk home. I don't wish to impose," Artemis said.

"Not at all. Besides, I'm sure Joey would like to see you again." Steve gestured to the back of the truck. "With Joey lying down up front there's not much room, but there's padding in the flat bed. How far's your house?"

"Couple miles up the road," Artemis said.

Steve nodded. "It's settled, then."

Steve opened the tailgate, and was surprised at Artemis's quickness as he hopped aboard. Climbing back in the cab, Steve opened the rear window.

"My name's Steve and this is my wife, Kate. Of course, you already know Joey."

Joey craned his neck to look out the window. "Hi, Artemis," he said.

"Hey there, buddy." Artemis smiled at the boy and then settled back for the ride.

CHAPTER FOUR

Steve turned on the radio, trying to force the real purpose of this trip out of his thoughts. He looked on as Kate stroked Joey's head.

He looked at the rear view mirror to see Artemis with his head tilted toward the sky, eyes closed, smiling as the sun bathed his face. Steve smiled back at the mirror before looking ahead to the road. They were approaching the dunes bordering the water.

The salty smell of the ocean, carried by sea breeze, now filled the air. Steve inhaled deeply, the smell bringing back memories of happier times.

"My house is up the road just a bit. Maybe you'd like to stop by the cove. Joey can look out to the sea," Artemis offered through the window.

Steve and Kate exchanged looks.

"We were planning on getting Joey home," Steve said, though he wondered what harm would be done if they stayed for a few minutes.

Artemis nodded. "I understand."

"Daddy, I'd like to see the ocean. Can't we stop?" Joey asked.

Kate nodded to Steve.

"Sure, we can. Artemis, let me know when we're getting close," Steve said.

After a few minutes, Artemis directed Steve to turn off of the paved highway. He drove onto a sandy path cutting through a vine-laden stand of sumac and pine. Steve followed the winding, jasmine-scented trail until the cries of the gulls and breaking waves sounded from close by.

Suddenly, the path opened wide. They were on a small, narrow beach of a tiny inlet. Palm trees had replaced pines, as tiny waves lapped the pinkish shoreline just a few feet beyond the shade of the trees. It was a beautiful spot.

Steve, Kate, and Joey just stared through the windshield.

CHAPTER FIVE

"I sure do like it here," Artemis said. "Sometimes, I just come down and forget to leave."

Chuckling, he climbed down from the truck bed and stood next to Steve's door. He'd already taken off his shoes and wiggled his toes in the sand.

"Can't say I'd blame you for that," Steve answered, as he and Kate got out of the truck. Steve walked around and carried Joey out of the passenger door.

"Can I put my feet in the water, Dad?" Joey asked.

"Well, sure!" Steve answered.

Steve picked a shady spot on the soft sand and lowered Joey down. He slowly removed the layer of blankets, looking at the skinny body underneath. He knew Joey was watching him, so he made the effort not to wince at the heartbreaking sight.

The boy weighed as much as an average three-year-old. Only a few wisps of his hair remained. His face was swollen from fluid buildup. He had the look all too common in the terminally ill: the bulging, jaundiced eyes, the pained expression, arms and legs like lesion-covered sticks.

Steve took off his own shoes and rolled up his pants. Kate did the same. Together, they brought Joey to the water's edge, allowing the warm waves to lap their feet. The water was like a clear, liquid jade. Little fish swam in the shallows while a crab did an underwater sidestep routine.

Artemis joined them in the water. "If we're lucky, my friends will show up soon."

"Your friends?" Kate asked.

Artemis beamed. "My friends."

He pointed to the open water toward the reef, where the waves churned white foam beyond the calm of the cove. He pointed to three dorsal fins breaking the surface in the shallows.

"They're never far away," he said.

Steve and Kate were alarmed, but relaxed when Joey said, "Dolphins!"

CHAPTER SIX

Artemis waded out further, laughing aloud as the dolphins swam excitedly around him. He patted their sleek skin as the creatures clicked and whirred their greetings.

"They just started showing up one day," he said. "I used to feed them sometimes. But they don't really seem to care much about food."

"They're wild dolphins?" Steve asked. He was amazed at the sight.

Artemis nodded. "Well, far as I can tell, yes. But as smart as they are, they seem tame."

"Can I pet one?" Joey whispered, wanting more than anything to touch his favorite animal in the world.

"I don't know." Kate's maternal instinct spoke up.

Steve looked at her. "It's okay, Hon. We'll be right next to him. Look how gentle they are."

They watched as the dolphins took turns raising their heads from the water, with Artemis whispering and gently petting them.

Looking up, he waved the family over. "Bring Joey here. They want to meet him."

Steve carried Joey deeper, with Kate right next to them.

Artemis spoke soothingly to the dolphins. They turned quickly, swimming over to the family, allowing the strangers to pet them.

Suddenly, their clicks and squeaks stopped. They nuzzled Joey gently, as they would one of their own newborns. The dolphins seemed to be studying him, confused. One began to make a noise like it was crying. The others soon echoed the haunting sound.

Joey didn't seem to care, running his fingers over their smooth, warm skin. His smile stretched ear to ear. This was about as happy as he'd ever been.

Artemis waded over, whispering in Steve's ear. "They know he's sick. It's upsetting them. That's why they're making those sounds."

"Should we take him out?" Steve asked.

Artemis shook his head. "No. Let him enjoy himself. They don't mind him being here. They just feel bad that he's sick."

Steve looked him in the eye. "How do you know this?"

Solemnly, Artemis looked down at the dolphins nuzzling the boy. "I just know."

CHAPTER SEVEN

The dolphins soon quieted down, though they stayed close to Joey. Kate and Steve were enjoying themselves for the first time in years, more so because their son was happier than they'd ever seen him.

A half hour had passed when the dolphins began to circle wider and wider, until they disappeared into deeper water. Steve and Kate carried their smiling son to the soft sand, where they sat down as Artemis joined them.

"What did you think of that, Joey?" Artemis asked, beaming again. "Not many people get to see dolphins up close."

"They're the best!" Joey said.

Artemis nodded. "Yes, they are."

After an hour, Steve and Kate decided it was time to leave. They looked at Joey, sleeping peacefully on a blanket in the shade.

"I hope this wasn't too much for him," Kate said.

"Are you kidding? Look how he's sleeping. No thrashing, no feverish, delirious fits. This was great for him." Steve looked at Artemis. "Thank you for letting our son enjoy himself so much..."

His voice trailed off and he lowered his head. Kate put a hand on her husband's shoulder, joining him in silence.

Artemis looked at the sleeping child, then out to sea. "Well, now you know where this place is. Stop by anytime you'd like. My house is up the path a stretch," he said.

"If Joey's up to the drive, we'll be back soon," Steve said. He imagined his son's smiling face as he petted the dolphins.

Kate hugged Artemis, with Steve following her.

"If I'm not here when you come back, just tell my son that Poppy said it was all right."

Artemis winked at the couple and watched as they gathered up their son and left.

Waving to them as they drove away, he looked out beyond the cove to the white breakers hitting the reef. After a few moments, he turned and walked slowly up the path leading to his house.

CHAPTER EIGHT

Joey slept for the entire ride home. He didn't wake up when the truck stopped. Steve carried him into his room and lowered him onto the bed.

Kate was there to wash him and change his pajamas. She opened the blanket. "Steve... Look at his arms!" she said.

Steve spun toward the bed. The lesions on Joey's arms had faded. Not believing what he saw, Steve turned on the table lamp. His eyes were not playing tricks.

Kate and Steve exchanged looks of shock.

"How can this be?" Kate asked.

Joey's eyes blinked open and he yawned.

"Where are we?" he asked.

"We're in your bedroom, son," Steve said. "How are you feeling?"

Joey looked around the room. Slowly, he recognized the stuffed animals and the airplane model hanging from the ceiling.

"I remember now." He smiled suddenly. "Those dolphins were cool!"

Kate and Steve laughed. There was life in their son's eyes now, clear and bright.

"Mommy, can I have a drink?" Joey asked.

"Of course, sweetheart."

As Kate moved quickly to the kitchen, Steve watched his son's face. It was hard to pinpoint, but Joey looked a hundred times better than he had that morning at the hospital.

It wasn't just his eyes and the faded lesions, but also the firmer skin with healthier coloring. Not once had he mentioned pain. Normally, he didn't say anything, but his parents could tell he was hurting. But that clearly wasn't the case now.

Kate came back with ginger ale, which Joey drank quickly through a straw. Joey raised his arms, turning them side to side, studying them in the lamplight.

"Mom?" he asked.

"Yes, Joey?" Kate answered.

"Can I have a banana?" Joey asked.

The rest of Joey's first night home went infinitely better than Steve and Kate could have hoped. Joey ate more food than they'd ever seen him eat. He then went back to that deep, restful sleep.

CHAPTER NINE

That night, Steve and Kate stayed with their son in his room. They talked about Joey's improvement, whether it was simply the child's happiness about leaving the hospital, or the joy of playing with the dolphins. Whatever the reason, they were thankful.

"I think we should take Joey back to the cove," Steve blurted out. "He was much better after we visited there. Let's go back. There's a motel just up the highway where we can stay."

"But Steve, remember the reason we brought him home," Kate said.

"Well, the doctors wanted to give up, but I don't! Let's see how he feels in the morning. Besides, Kate..." gently, Steve held his wife in his arms, "don't you remember how we felt today while we were there? We've never had that before. I want it again."

Kate studied her husband's face, nodding with his words. She also wanted more of those moments. She'd never seen her son smile so much. And now, they could have another day together as a family. Maybe more than one day.

Joey awoke to the peep of the birds the next morning. He saw his parents asleep on the loveseat near his bed, Kate's head resting on Steve's shoulder. He propped himself up on an elbow. "Mom?"

Kate opened her eyes. "How are you feeling?" she asked. She saw that Joey leaned on his elbow. "The doctors said you'd hurt your arms doing that."

Even in the dim light, she could see the color in his cheeks. She kissed his head, then looked closely at his arms. The lesions had faded even more. His skin glowed with life under her fingers as she touched him.

"I'm hungry," he said, without hesitation.

After breakfast, they packed a few bags and headed out in the truck. Propped up by a few pillows, Joey could sit upright in the seat, looking at sights he'd normally miss. He was really looking forward to the cove and, hope-fully, the dolphins.

CHAPTER TEN

They followed the path where Artemis had directed them the day before. Joey looked over the dashboard, his hopeful eyes scanning the shimmering water. Steve and Kate silently marveled at their son's appearance, wondering what this new day would bring.

Steve carried Joey to the water. They waded out, soaking in the warming caress of the sun and the ocean.

Joey spoke. "Dad, I want to stand... myself."

Steve lowered the boy until his feet touched bottom. Leaning on his father's arm,

Joey stood on his own. He splashed water onto his face with his free hand, laughing out loud.

"Look out there!" Kate called out, pointing to the sea.

The dolphins were back. Three dorsal fins skimmed happily through the water toward the family.

Without the benefit of Artemis's calming presence, Steve and Kate cringed a bit. They were uneasy with the large creatures swimming within reach. But Joey held out his hands as the dolphins circled around. They seemed to recognize him, from the happy sound of their clicks and whistles.

Though they stayed near Joey, the dolphins did not repeat their sad sounds from the day before. Joey smiled in the happiness of his connection with nature. After all those days of pain, it was the simplest pleasures of life that he now treasured most in the world.

Later that morning, Joey's parents checked into the nearby motel. For the next week, they brought him back every day to the cove and the dolphins. As the days passed, he grew stronger. The lesions disappeared from his skin, and his scalp darkened as hair began to grow again. He could walk, laugh, even climb on his father's back for a ride.

Though Steve and Kate didn't know what the future might hold for their child, his healing had given them hope. Hope that, God willing, the doctors had all been wrong with their sad news.

CHAPTER ELEVEN

They had stopped at Artemis's house every day, but he was never home. His son wasn't there, either. They wrote him a nice letter and slipped it under the front door.

Steve thought about going to the hospital to see Artemis there while he was working, but he decided against bringing Joey back there. So on their last night in the motel, they went back to the house one last time, hoping to see their friend.

Steve drove up the driveway. Since it was already dark, he noticed the lights were on in the house.

"Looks like someone's here," he said.

There was a pickup truck like theirs parked in the driveway. As Steve pulled behind it, a man looked out the window.

They approached the front steps. The door was opened by a younger, taller, unsmiling version of Artemis.

"Yes?" the man asked.

"We were hoping that Artemis was in," Steve said.

The man nodded. "Are you the folks who left the letter?"

"Yes, we are," Steve said.

The man waved them in. "Why don't you come inside?"

As they entered the living room the man gestured for them to sit on the sofa. He introduced himself as Jeremy. Steve noticed the framed pictures of Artemis and Jeremy adorning the walls.

"Is Artemis here? Will he be home soon?" Steve asked.

Jeremy didn't answer right away. He seemed to be at a loss for words.

"I'm not sure who you spoke with," he finally said. "But it couldn't have been my father."

Kate shook her head. "But he's in the pictures here on the wall," she said.

"It couldn't have been my father," Jeremy said again.

A strange feeling came over Steve. He said, "He told us to tell you that Poppy said it was okay if we swam at the cove."

Jeremy now seemed completely confused, shaking his head. "No one knows that I called him Poppy," he said. "No one."

Steve and Kate looked at each other. Even Joey knew something was up.

Jeremy looked at the family in front of him. "Look," he said. "My father died two years ago."

CHAPTER TWELVE

Steve felt icy fingers on his neck. So did Kate.

"This isn't the first time someone's come here and told me they've seen him," Jeremy said. He stood, facing the window to look out at the dark trees. "He worked at the hospital. Loved kids. They loved him back." He paused, and the silence was uncomfortable. "Since he died, there's always been someone with a kid from the hospital who's claimed to have seen him."

The three adults looked at each other.

Finally, Kate spoke. "He was with us, Jeremy. I hugged him. We both did! The dolphins even swam with him."

Steve nodded. He repeated the entire story of Joey's illness and healing, of Artemis's kindness, of their interaction with the dolphins.

"He was with us at the cove," he said. "And he suggested we should come back. When we left after our first visit, he was still there."

Jeremy finally smiled, though sadly. "He loved the cove. That was his favorite place on this earth."

Joey had listened to all of this. Death was no stranger to him, close as he'd been to dying.

"He's here with us right now," he said.

The grownups turned to him.

"I know what I felt inside when he was near me. I felt warmth, and I feel that right now."

Joey looked at Artemis's son, with his skeptical expression. "Maybe you need to believe he's here to see him, Jeremy."

Jeremy looked away from the boy and around the room. Many times, he thought he'd seen a shadow out of the corner of his eye. When he'd turn his head, the shadow would vanish.

But he didn't believe in the afterlife. He never shared his father's faith. There had been a few dreams where Artemis had appeared and talked to him. But Jeremy would always wake up to his own dark room and silence.

But these people were too honest. They had information no one else could possibly know. Maybe this was his father's way of communicating with him.

Maybe if he did believe, and loved life with a child's heart again, he'd be able to see more. Looking at the boy, Jeremy smiled.

"He was a good man," he said. "No doubt he'd be a good soul."

"An angel's more like it," said Joey.

The three grownups exchanged looks, nodding with the wisdom of the child's words.

CHAPTER THIRTEEN

The atmosphere of the room lightened. The family stayed and chatted with Jeremy until Joey finally fell asleep against Kate's shoulder. As they were leaving, with Steve carrying his sleeping son, he and Kate told Jeremy that they wanted to stay in touch.

Jeremy nodded, truly touched, finally beaming a smile that rivaled his father's. He waved to the family as they drove away down the dark driveway.

Back inside the house, Jeremy looked at the photos on the wall. They were the memories of his life with Artemis, whose company he surely missed.

Maybe he had to say those words aloud.

"Poppy, if you can hear me, then I want you to know that I do miss you… more than you can know," he said.

The house remained quiet. After a while, Jeremy decided to walk down to the cove that Artemis had loved so much. Maybe he'd see dolphins swimming by moonlight, or a shadow out of the corner of his eye.

He strolled barefoot through the cool sand, inhaling deeply of the sweet jasmine scent. Reaching down at the surf's edge, he scooped some water and splashed his face.

The moonlight reflected softly upon the water. He remembered coming down here with his father at night as a kid. Sometimes they'd listen to the waves. Other times, Artemis would talk about the past, or the hopes he had for Jeremy's future.

Jeremy noticed the dolphins had entered the cove, their fins skimming towards him. He waded out farther and the dolphins greeted him as a long-lost friend. Indeed, he was, since he hadn't done this in two years.

As he ran his hands over their smooth skin, something made him look back to the water's edge. Near the spot he'd just left was the shadow of a man. But this time, it didn't disappear.

Unafraid, Jeremy took a few steps towards shore. "Poppy?"

A moment passed. Then the smile beaming back through the night gave him his answer.

About the Author

Leonard Varasano is a contributing author to the Storyshares library.

About the Publisher

Storyshares is a publisher focused on supporting the millions of teens and adults who struggle with reading by creating a new shelf in the library specifically for them. The ever-growing collection features content that is compelling and culturally relevant for teens and adults, yet still readable at a range of lower reading levels.

Storyshares generates content by engaging deeply with writers, bringing together a community to create this new kind of book. With more intriguing and approachable stories to choose from, the teens and adults who have fallen behind are improving their skills and beginning to discover the joy of reading.
For more information, visit storyshares.org.

Easy to Read. Hard to Put Down.